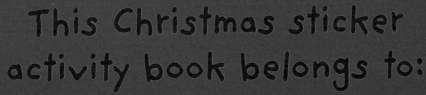

This Christmas sticker activity book belongs to:

....

Pets love Christmas, too!
Color in this Christmas scene.

Trace the little reindeer and color him in!

Can you find the shiny red nose on the sticker pages for him?

Decorate the sleigh
and add as many present
stickers as you can!

Decorate your own Christmas card using stickers and crayons.

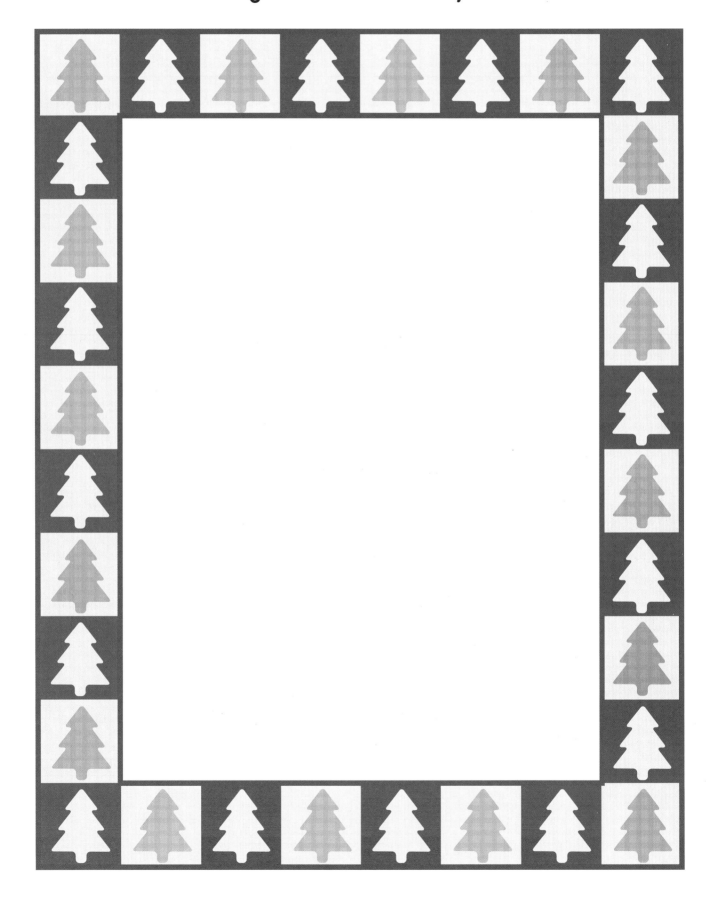

Who threw the snowball? Follow the trails to find out which elf hit the window.

What's in the snowglobe? You decide! Don't forget to add sparkly snowflake stickers.

Draw a little bird sitting in the window.

Find some stickers of sweet treats to decorate these gingerbread men and Christmas cookies.

Decorate your own
wrapping paper
for a friend's
Christmas present!

Can you find some snowy animal friends on the sticker pages for Polar Bear and Penguin?

Can you find five differences between these smiley snowmen?

Santa's elves have mixed up the mail!
Find the envelope stickers that are the same color
as the trays and put them in the right trays.

Trace Santa, his bag, and
the pile of presents.

Then use your crayons and
stickers to decorate them.

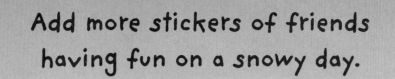

Add more stickers of friends
having fun on a snowy day.

This little elf is
thinking of all the toys
he wants for Christmas!
Can you color them in?

Can you
find five
differences
between
these elves?

Follow the green trail to find out which present is for this little mouse.

A

B

C

Make a "STOP HERE, SANTA" sign and decorate it with stickers.

Trace the dotted lines to finish these pictures, then color them in.

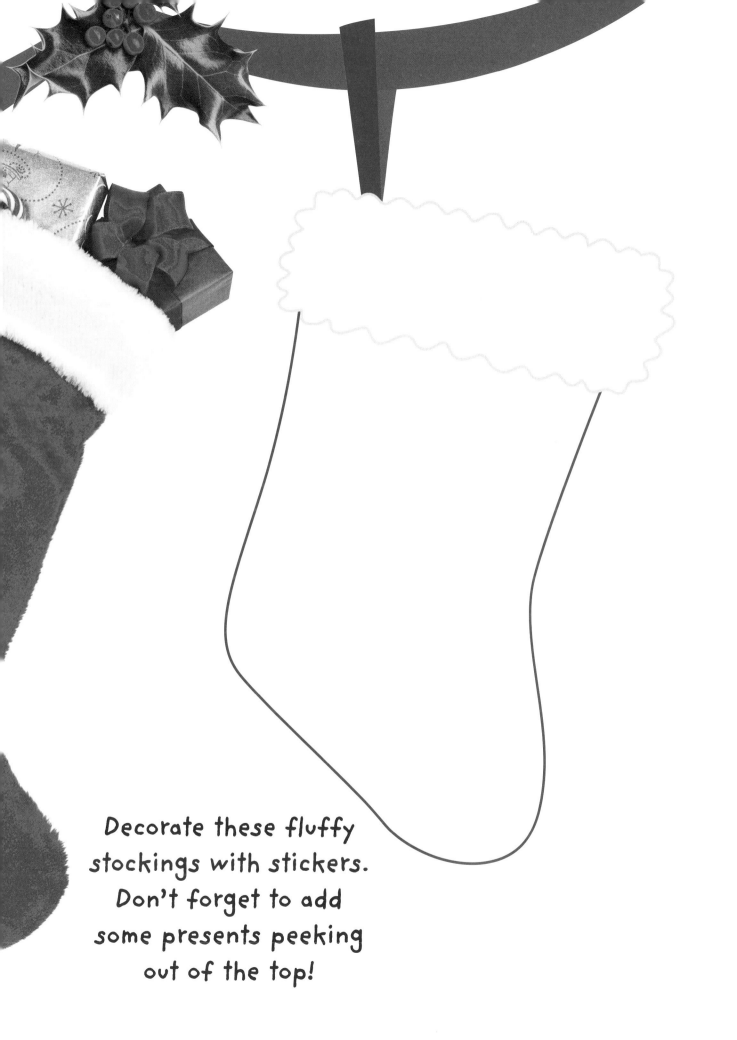

Decorate these fluffy
stockings with stickers.
Don't forget to add
some presents peeking
out of the top!

Decorate the Christmas tree with lots of bright and festive stickers! Add stocking stickers to the fireplace.

Connect the dots to find out what this little girl wants for Christmas.